These stickers are just for you!

Dear Parent,

Sharing a book is the perfect opportunity to get close and cuddle with your child. Research has shown that reading aloud to and with your child is probably the single most important thing you can do to prepare him or her for success in school. When you share a book with your child, not only are you helping to strengthen his or her reading and vocabulary skills, you are also stimulating your child's curiosity, imagination and enthusiasm for reading.

Join Winnie the Pooh and his friends from the Hundred-Acre Wood as they discover things that make each one of them special and unique. Invite your child to name qualities that he or she possesses that make him or her truly special and one-of-a-kind. Being able to connect with a story by identifying with the characters, and thinking about personal experiences that are similar, is an important strategy that enables readers to more fully understand and engage with the story.

Children learn in different ways and at different speeds. Remember, successful readers have one thing in common: supportive, loving adults who share books with them often, to nurture a lifelong love of books, reading and learning.

Enjoy your reading adventure together!

First published by Parragon in 2012
Parragon
Chartist House
15–17 Trim Street
Bath BA1 1HA, UK
www.parragon.com

Consultants: Cheryl Stroud, English Language Arts Curriculum Leader and Reading Specialist,
Concord Road Elementary School, Ardsley, NY; Beth Sycamore, Literacy Consultant, Chicago, IL

Editor: Joëlle Murphy

Designer: Scott Petrower

Illustrated by the Disney Storybook Artists

ISBN 978-1-78186-023-6

Printed in China

I Love ...

Bath · New York · Singapore · Hong Kong · Cologne · Delhi
Melbourne · Amsterdam · Johannesburg · Shenzhen

My eyes.

My ears.

My legs.

My nose.

My mouth.

My tummy.

My honey!

Make: A paper you!

You will need:

- Butcher paper (a large roll of paper found in craft shops)
- Crayons or markers
- Scissors
- Tissue paper or newspaper
- Stapler
- Clothes that fit you

Craft materials may stain – take care to cover clothing and furnishings.

Instructions:

1. Place two layers of butcher paper on the ground and lie down on them. Ask a grown-up to trace around your body onto the paper.

2. Ask an adult to cut out the shape. You now have *two* pieces shaped like you!

3. Staple the pieces together around the top half only, then draw your face, eyes, hair, mouth and nose on one side.

4. Gently stuff the shapes with newspaper then finish stapling them together. Now dress your paper doll in your favourite clothes!

Make: A photo puzzle

Materials:

- 10cm x 15cm photo of YOU
- 10cm x 15cm piece of cardboard
- Glue
- Scissors

Instructions:

1. Ask a grown-up to help you glue the photo to the cardboard. Let it dry.

2. Ask a grown-up to cut the photograph into four or more square pieces.

3. Turn the pieces over and mix them up. Now try to put yourself together!

My Special Things

I like my house.

I like my bed.

I like my rug.

I like my table.

I like my chair.

I like my honey.

I like me!

A special place for me

Pooh loves his home and all the things inside that make it special. Now you can make a door hanger to hang on the door of your favourite place in your house!

Ask a grown-up to help you cut out the door hanger along the pink lines. Make sure to cut the inner circle and the slit at the top, so it can easily slip over a door handle.

Colour and decorate both sides of your door hanger with pictures of you or your favourite things, and slip your door hanger on the door of your special spot!

Hooray!

Tigger can bounce.

Hooray for Tigger!

Rabbit can cook.

Hooray for Rabbit!

Eeyore can float.

Hooray for Eeyore!

You can read.
Hooray for you!

Well done! Sticker Book

Pooh and his friends can do some very special things. You can make a sticker book to remember their talents. Ask a grown-up to cut out the pages of the book below, following the pink dotted lines. Lay pages 4 and 5 on top of pages 2 and 3 of the sticker book. Fold the book in half along the blue lines and staple the pages together.

Look at the names on each page, and match the stickers on your sticker sheet to the correct name. On the last page, draw a picture of YOU doing something special. Don't forget to write what you can do!

When you are finished, find someone you can read your book to.

Owl can read. Well done!

1

Eeyore can build. Well done!

3

I can _____. Well done!

8

© Disney

Pooh can sweep. Well done!

6 © Disney

Tigger can bounce. Well done!

Piglet can swing. Well done!

Rabbit can dig. Well done!

Roo can wash. Well done!